Shaun Shoots the Sheep
and
Camping Chaos

EGMONT

We bring stories to life

First published in Great Britain 2009
by Egmont UK Limited
239 Kensington High Street, London W8 6SA

Text by Beth Harwood. Based on original storylines by
Lee Pressman and Julie Jones.

© and ™ Aardman Animations Ltd. 2009. All rights reserved.
Based on a character created by Nick Park.
Developed by Richard (Golly) Goleszowksi with Alison Snowden and David Fine.

ISBN 978 1 4052 4451 0
1 3 5 7 9 10 8 6 4 2

Printed in Italy

FSC
Mixed Sources
Product group from well-managed
forests and other controlled sources
Cert no. TT-COC-002332
www.fsc.org
© 1996 Forest Stewardship Council

Egmont is passionate about helping to preserve the world's remaining ancient forests.
We only use paper from legal and sustainable forest sources.

This book is made from paper certified by the Forestry Stewardship Council (FSC),
an organisation dedicated to promoting responsible management of forest resources.
For more information on the FSC, please visit www.fsc.org. To learn more about
Egmont's sustainable paper policy, please visit www.egmont.co.uk/ethical

Shaun Shoots the Sheep
and
Camping Chaos

2 baa-rilliant stories as seen on TV!

Contents

Shaun Shoots the Sheep

Contents

Camping Chaos

Shaun Shoots the Sheep

Adapted from the original episode written by Lee Pressman

Chapter 1
Lost Property

It was just another day on the farm. The sun was out, the sky was cloudless.

The sheep were grazing peacefully as Bitzer sat beneath a shady tree, supposedly keeping watch.

Suddenly, the flock heard *SCHLUMP-SCHLUMP-SCHLUMP-SCHLUMP!*

The peace was broken by the sound of boots walking across soggy grass. Shaun looked up and bleated a curious "Meh?"

A cheery man and lady had climbed over the stile into the field. The man wore neat round glasses. He carried an enormous backpack. The lady carried a heavy shoulder bag that bulged peculiarly. Shaun wondered what was inside. Lots of spare woolly socks, maybe?

The happy hikers hummed as they crossed the field. They stopped by Bitzer, and the lady gasped at the sight of such an adorable dog. She reached into her shoulder bag and pulled out a shiny silver box.

Now, *this* was interesting. Shaun narrowed his eyes and shuffled closer.

The lady passed the silver box to the man. He plucked off his glasses and held the box to his face. Bitzer growled warily. *What's going on?*

The man pushed a red button on top of the box. The box went CLICK! Then WHIRR! A flash of light made Bitzer's eyes water.

A moment later, a piece of paper popped out of the silver box.

The hikers peered at the piece of paper. They seemed very pleased with what was on it – a picture of Bitzer. To the hikers, he was a model mutt!

The lady reached into her pocket and pulled out a chicken drumstick. Bitzer's face lit up and he begged for his reward. He grabbed the drumstick and with a slobbery *SLURRRRRRRP*, he gulped down the meat in one!

Then Bitzer scampered round the back of the farmhouse, and Shaun heard the scrabble of his paws in the earth as he buried the bone. Bitzer was very secretive about where he hid his bones. Shaun wasn't sure why. The flock would never want to pinch them . . . except for Shirley, who would eat just about anything!

The field gate creaked as the hikers climbed over it. But as the lady clambered up and over, the silver box tumbled out of her bag and landed softly on the grass.

Shaun watched as the hikers strode up the hill. They didn't notice their precious box was missing.

But Shaun certainly did!

Chapter 2
Snap-Happy Shaun

Shaun didn't miss a bleat. He snatched up the box and held it to his face – the wrong way round. His hoof clipped the button and a flash of light stunned him.

Shaun realised what was going on. The box was a camera! He'd seen the Farmer with a camera before, taking pictures of his niece playing not so nicely. But this camera was a lot more fun – the pictures popped out straight away! Shaun had fancied himself as a photographer ever since – and now his chance had come!

WHIRRRRR! went the camera. Shaun blinked his throbbing eyes. A piece of paper popped out of the camera, and hung there like a daft, droopy tongue.

Slowly, a picture appeared on it. It was an extreme close-up of a big, brown, sheepy-looking eye.

Shaun took one look and tossed it aside. He could do better than that! He glanced around the farm, looking for something that would make a good photo. He saw the flock in front of him, watching with interest as he played with his new toy. "Yehhh!" Shaun bleated. He could take a group shot – a fleecy family portrait!

Every sheep had a big grin. They all

wanted to pose for Shaun! He moved the camera about, trying to capture the whole flock at once, but they wouldn't all fit in the viewfinder window!

Snap-happy Shaun waved his hoof at the flock. *Move in closer! Huddle up!* In a thundering of hooves and a flurry of fleece, they bustled together and bleated.

Ready when you baa!

Shaun peered through the tiny viewfinder window.

He saw Shirley first of all. She filled the window by herself.

On Shirley's back was a sheep.

No . . . Two sheep.

No . . . Three sheep! Four sheep! Even more sheep! The whole flock was balanced on poor old Shirley!

Shaun lifted the camera and followed the tower of sheep to the very top. There stood Timmy on his mother's back!

This will never do!

Shaun scratched his head and came up with a better idea. He waved his hoof towards the ground. *Down a bit!*

The flock tumbled to the ground like woolly hay bales and posed again for Shaun. When Shaun peered through the viewfinder, he saw a perfect formation of grinning sheep, standing four-in-a-row on each other's backs.

Maa-vellous!

But as he pressed the red button to take the shot, a rubber plunger full of gooey gum soared over the sheep, and stuck to the camera – *SHHHLOP!*

"Mehhh!" cried Shaun, as the camera flew out of his hooves and into a pair of waiting trotters . . .

. . . belonging to the Naughty Pigs! They'd seen Shaun's new toy and wanted it for themselves!

With a *BAA-HUFF,* Shaun hoofed it over to the pigsty wall. But he was too late. Those pigs were already hogging his camera! In a flurry of clicks, whirrs, flashes and grunts, their photoshoot was well underway. They grimaced and gurned, preened and posed, shimmied and strutted – and soon had a gallery of gruesome pig-tures!

Shaun shook his head. This wasn't on!

He'd get that camera back by hook or by crook . . . and he'd start with a hook!

He trotted into the barn and returned with a fishing rod. He crouched behind the wall and dangled the fishing line into the pigsty, guessing by the grunts where the camera might be.

He felt a tug. *Bingo!* He'd hooked the camera. He began to reel in his catch. The camera rose out of the Naughty Pig's trotters, but the stubborn swine grabbed hold of the gadget and tugged hard.

Shaun yanked and pulled from the other side, but the pig was too strong. The pig tugged on the fishing line and in a bleating, blurry arc of wool, Shaun flew over the wall, landing headfirst in pigswill on the other side!

With a click and a squeal of glee, the pigs made sure to take a photo of Shaun's messy landing.

Chapter 3
Bitzer, the Great Dog-tective

From deep beneath the earth, within his secret stash of bones, Bitzer heard a familiar whistle.

"Phoo-witt!"

It could only be the Farmer! *What now?* growled Bitzer as he scampered to the surface – no longer a mutt of mystery, but Man's Best Friend.

Bitzer trotted to his master's side and saluted obediently as the Farmer patted his head. Then the Farmer began to swing an empty shoulder bag back and forth in front of Bitzer's nose. The dog gave the bag a bored sort of sniff – what was he supposed to be sniffing for? But as the Farmer moved the bag away, Bitzer found himself looking into the hopeful eyes of the man with the glasses and the very nice lady with the scrummy chicken drumstick! They'd lost their camera and traced their route back to the farm, hoping Bitzer could sniff it out.

Bitzer had a sudden thought. If he found the camera, he'd get another bone!

He gave the lady's shoulder bag a good, heavy sniff, and off he went on his mission.

Bitzer scurried around the field, sniffing the ground, dodging the droppings, tracking the scent of the missing camera.

Suddenly – *aha!* Bitzer found a clue. He felt like a proper dog-tective – like Sherlock Bones! He held up the evidence and looked at it under a magnifying glass.

It was a photo of an eye. A big, brown, sheepy-looking eye!

Bitzer was definitely on to something.

With his nose to the ground, he scampered around until he found another clue. This time, a photo of a tower of sheep with a rubber plunger flying overhead!

Bitzer growled, feeling annoyed. *What have those sheep been up to now?* He had to find that camera. *Camera equals bone!* He could almost taste his reward!

But it wouldn't be as easy as he thought . . .

The sheep themselves were hard to miss. Still piled high, they were watching the antics in the pigsty.

But there was no sign of the camera.

A startled bleat from behind the wall got Bitzer's attention.

"Meeeehhh!" cried Shaun, as he was tossed from trotter to trotter. Somehow he had become the ball in the Naughty Pigs' game of Piggy in the Middle!

Shaun appeared, then dropped behind the wall one last time.

The flock's ears pricked up nervously, listening for a baa.

But there was silence.

What had happened to Shaun?

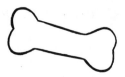

Chapter 4
Shaun 1, Naughty Pigs 0

The flock looked at one another and at Bitzer, their eyes big with worry.

Suddenly, a muddy hoof appeared over the wall. A bedraggled Shaun pulled himself up and gave a weary wave.

"Mehhh!" the flock cheered.

With a loud "Oink!" the pigs yanked Shaun back into the sty. But Shaun was soon fighting hoof and nail to get away. After a few more rounds of Sheepy in the

Middle, he threw himself over the wall, landing *THWUMP!* on his bottom!

But wait . . . What had fallen into his flailing hoof as he landed?

Shaun was muddy, bruised and battered, but he'd rescued the camera! With a "Baa!" of triumph, he held it up for the flock to see.

The sheep cheered loudly and Bitzer's eyes lit up. *Camera equals bone*, he thought greedily.

The flock pulled their cheesiest grins as Shaun waved them closer together. Suddenly, a paw reached out and snatched the camera.

Bitzer! *Trust him to spoil their fun!*

Shaun trotted after Bitzer and called him

back. If Bitzer wanted to take the camera, couldn't he take a picture first?

Bitzer looked at the battle-worn Shaun and decided to do him a favour. After all, he had a reward waiting back at the farmhouse, and he started slobbering at the very thought of another tasty drumstick!

Shaun took his place at the front of the flock, and the sheep grinned and posed.

Bitzer held up the camera and pressed the red button.

The camera clicked, flashed . . . and gave a pathetic *whirr-umph*.

Nothing popped out.

Bitzer gave the camera a shake and held it to his ear. Still nothing.

The camera was broken!

Bitzer gave a shrug. *Too bad!*

Off he ran with the camera between his teeth. He delivered it into the Farmer's hands and sat, waiting and panting, for his reward. All the effort had made Bitzer enormously hungry again!

The Farmer passed the camera back to the hikers. They were delighted to have it back, even if it did look worse for wear. The man wiped a blob of mud off with his finger, then aimed the camera at the Farmer. *"Say Cheese!"*

But vanity got the better of the Farmer, and before the man could press the button, he dashed into the farmhouse to smarten himself up.

The man took out a hanky and cleaned off the camera. It was absolutely clogged with mud!

Then – *WHIRRRRR!* went the camera.

Out popped a picture of a flock of sheep.

But this was no ordinary flock!

The woolly wonders were stacked one on top of the other in a neat formation with one ragged – yet cheeky – sheep right at the front, looking like the true leader of the flock!

Chapter 5
Picture Perfect!

Shaun had been comforting the poor forlorn flock, but they perked up when they heard the whirr of the camera. Was it working again?

Still in formation, they scurried behind the wall and peered over the shoulders of the hikers. The hikers did not suspect a thing . . . until Shaun's little black hoof plucked the photograph out of the lady's hand.

The hikers turned around. To their utter shock, they saw the flock admiring their own portrait. Slowly they backed away looking ever so slightly worried.

They're not scared of sheep, are they? Shaun chuckled as he watched them.

Apparently they were. These were like no other sheep they had ever known!

The man and his wife sidestepped away. They gave a small sheepish smile then ran for the hills, taking their camera with them.

Bitzer sat outside the farmhouse, moping. *So much for my great reward,* he whined, as his dreams of another juicy bone disappeared.

The farmhouse door flew open. Out stepped the Farmer, ready for his close-up. He'd combed his hair, polished his glasses and put on his best sweater and spotty bow tie. He was beaming from ear to ear with pride in his fine appearance.

But he soon stopped smiling when he realised the hikers had gone! *How rude!* He tore off his bow tie, tossed it over his shoulder and stomped back into the farmhouse with an angry grunt, slamming the door behind him.

Bitzer sniffed at the bow tie and snapped it up in his jaws. He chewed it thoughtfully. It squeaked in his mouth.

Bitzer cheered up. The bow tie was not as juicy as a bone, but it *looked* quite like a bone and was much more fun!

That night, the barn echoed with the sound of hammering. Shaun bashed the last nail into the photograph to hang it on the wall. It now had a smart gold frame around it.

Shaun stood back to admire his work and bleated happily.

The flock joined in with a chorus of contented bleats as they admired themselves in the fabulous, fleecy family portrait!

Shaun Shoots the Sheep

The happy hikers!

"Say Cheese!"

Shaun attempts to shoot the sheep . . .

Shaun's new toy is snatched from his hooves!

A gallery of gruesome pig-tures!

Bitzer, the Great Dog-tective.

"Camera equals bone . . ." Bitzer gives in to greed.

Shaun and the hikers admire the flock's fleecy portrait!

Camping Chaos

A tent's moment for Bitzer and Shaun.

"Go fetch!"

Shaun ventures inside the tent.

Timmy's sausage skipping rope!

The sheep take shelter from the rain.

The Camper discovers the intruders!

The Camper resurrects his tent.

Shaun and Bitzer's revenge!

Camping Chaos

Adapted from the original episode written by Julie Jones

Chapter 1
A Gruesome Guest

There was no such thing as an ordinary day on the farm.

Shaun and the flock knew to expect the unexpected – though, so far, everything that morning had gone according to plan.

Breakfast? Check.

Sheep dip? Check.

Round-up? Check.

Bitzer opened the gate. The flock barged through as he ticked them off his list.

Shaun led the sheep across the field, then stopped short with a startled "Maaaah?"

In the middle of the field was a great big tent! It looked to Shaun like a small, ugly barn made of bright orange cloth. It would be a tight squeeze for the flock to fit in it, Shaun thought to himself.

The other sheep bleated nervously. What was going on? Why was there a tent in their field? Shaun looked at Bitzer, but Bitzer didn't know either!

There were all sorts of bits and bobs around the tent – tins, packets, piles of twigs. Shaun frowned. Something wasn't right here. The field looked like a rubbish tip!

Bitzer and Shaun wandered over to take a closer look. The tent was pinned to the ground with pieces of rope, and Bitzer couldn't resist twanging one with his paw! Suddenly, they heard a noise from the front of the tent – a ZZZZZZZZIP – as a doorway opened up, and out came the face of a very grumpy man!

"Maaa!" cried Shaun, in surprise.

"Arroooo!" whined Bitzer, and the friends scuttled back to the flock.

They watched from a safe distance as the man stood up, stretched and slurped fizzy pop from a can with a revolting "GLUG-UG-UG!" noise. Then he gave a loud "BURRRRRP!" as he tossed the can across the field.

Shaun and Bitzer looked at one another.

Bitzer growled. *Right!* Something had

to be done about this nuisance camper! He decided to take matters into his own paws, and trotted over to confront the grumpy guest. *We're not having that! Off with you!* He yapped angrily, bouncing around him on all fours. Shaun was impressed. Bitzer was barking mad! The Camper scowled, and the flock's ears twitched in hope. Had Bitzer's barking scared him away?

The Camper bent down and picked up a stick. He waved it at Bitzer as if it were a magic wand. Sure enough, as if by magic, Bitzer stopped yapping.

Shaun covered his eyes and shook his head. This was not going well. Bitzer's eyes lit up and he begged for the stick, his tongue hanging out and his tail thwacking the ground happily. Shaun rolled his eyes.

Now they'd never be rid of the rubbish-throwing rotter!

The Camper tossed the stick across the field, knowing that Bitzer would scamper after it! Keen to impress his new friend, Bitzer took a long run-up and leapt into the air to catch the stick firmly in his teeth.

He padded back across the field, ready for another turn. The Camper was busy pulling a heavy rucksack on to his back, and he wanted the dog to leave him alone. He'd had his bit of fun. But as far as Bitzer was concerned, the Camper's games made him his new best friend!

The Camper patted Bitzer's head, snatched the stick and threw it far across the field. Maybe now the dratted dog would leave him alone!

But no.

Shaun and the flock watched with sinking hearts. Every time the Camper threw the stick, Bitzer ran to collect it and hurried back again. The Camper grew grumpier and grumpier! He wanted a peaceful walk, not a game of Fetch with an eager farm dog!

"Ner-ner-ner!" sang the Camper, as he waggled the stick above Bitzer's head. The dippy dog barked in great delight. Then the Camper hurled the stick over the stile, and Bitzer hurried after it. To Shaun's surprise, the Camper followed close behind.

Perhaps Bitzer isn't so daft after all, thought Shaun. He'd managed to get the grumpy Camper out of their field and off for a long, long walk!

Chapter 2
Shaun the Explorer

Now the coast was clear for the sheep to explore the tent. Shaun crawled in and poked around the muddy clothes and rusty lamps. But there didn't seem to be much to play with!

Suddenly, Shaun's nose wrinkled.

Something smelled BAD!

"Peeeoooo!" he bleated, wafting the stench away. He glanced around and soon found the cause – an old, soggy sock!

Shaun lifted it gingerly in one hoof and sniffed at it.

His head spun, his nose twitched. With a weak, wobbly "Maa . . .", the terrible pong from the sock made Shaun faint!

He teetered, toppled, and landed *PHHHWOOOOSH!* on a foot pump!

The foot pump was hooked up to a large inflatable mattress, and once he had recovered from the sock shock, Shaun found the pump was fun to bounce on!

HUFFA-PUFFA went the pump.

Shaun bounced again.

HUFFA-PUFFA.

HUFFA-PUFFA.

Shaun stood on the pump and hopped up and down. Meanwhile, the mattress grew bigger and bigger as it filled up with air!

HUFFA-PUFFA!

HUFFA-PUFFA!

HUFFA-PUFFA!

HUFFA-PUFFA!

The flock crowded round outside the tent, curious to know what Shaun was doing. One fearless sheep trotted forwards and poked his face in.

Suddenly – POP! The end of the pump fell out of the mattress!

It blew a very loud raspberry – PPPPPPPTTTHHHHHHHHHH – as the air squirted out. Shaun watched on as the mattress shot out of the tent, taking the unfortunate sheep with it! The sheep and the mattress flew round and round the field, as the air whooshed out of the nozzle where the pump had been attached.

After three more noisy circuits of the field, the poor sheep finally landed with a big KA-LUMPH head over hooves against the pigsty wall.

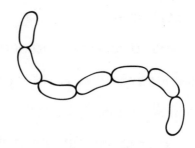

Chapter 3
Bangers and Mash!

The Naughty Pigs had heard the strange noises coming from the sheep field. They peered over the wall and saw the shell-shocked sheep lying beneath them, rolled up in the deflated mattress, his eyes spinning. Soon they were squealing with laughter!

Shaun poked his head out of the tent and frowned. What was going on?

But before he could find out, he caught

sight of something steaming. On the campfire was a potato, baking merrily away. It smelled scrummy!

Shaun licked his lips. He poked the potato with a twig, and plucked it off with his hoof. It was one seriously hot potato! "Ooh!" he gasped, tossing it from hoof to hoof. But it was much too hot! He threw it across the field to the flock. The sheep played 'keepy-uppy' with the steaming spud until it grew too hot for them and they tossed it into the air.

With a grace never seen before, Shirley, the biggest sheep of all, leapt up and caught the spud in her mouth before landing with a THUD. Shirley would never let food go to waste.

Shirley gave a loud GULP.

There was silence as she swallowed the red-hot potato, then . . . *WOOOOEEEEEEE!* Steam poured out of her ears and nose. It was too hot for even Shirley to handle!

Shaun was hungry. He flipped open the lid of a blue box left outside the tent. Was there food inside? He poked around and pulled out a sausage.

Then another.

And another

And *another!*

Shaun tugged at the string of sausages. It never seemed to end! The bangers kept coming and wouldn't break free from the box. Shaun was having his own Tug of War!

He squinted and strained, twisted and

tugged. Then, with a THWOP, the sausages came free and one by one the bangers landed on top of him!

Three of the sausages broke free mid-flight, and fell with a SPLAT on the pigsty wall. The Naughty Pigs had been watching the Sausage Tug of War and squealing with laughter. Suddenly, it didn't seem so funny.

The sausages were made of PORK!

The Naughty Pigs fainted into the mud with a squeal and a SPLOOSH! Moments later, a trembling trotter flicked the offending sausages away from them.

Shaun was still trapped under the bundle of bangers, as the sheep laughed and pointed. Summoning all his strength, Shaun pushed the string of sausages away.

It really was heavy! No wonder it hadn't snapped easily!

The Naughty Pigs recovered from their shock, and appeared, shuddering, behind the wall. The scene they saw would give them nightmares for months on end. Little Timmy was skipping with a string of sausages!

"EEEEEE!" squealed the Naughty Pigs in horror, fainting into the mud once more!

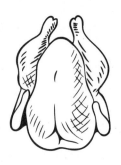

Chapter 4
In-tents Moments

The flock had totally forgotten the grumpy Camper. They were having far too much fun! Another sheep went into the tent and discovered a big, blue sleeping bag stuffed in one corner. She clutched the hem of the sleeping bag and tugged it over her head.

"Maaa!" she bleated in panic. She was well and truly stuck!

Shaun and the flock heard a CLUMPF.

The sleeping-bag-sheep wriggled out of the tent like a blue, fleecy caterpillar! She teetered and toppled, then fell headfirst into the box of food!

With a bleat of embarrassment, she tugged herself free, but her friends were in fits of giggles. The silly sheep had her head stuck in a raw chicken!

She gave a desperate bleat for help. But it was no use. The sight of a sheep dressed as a caterpillar with a chicken for a head was too funny! The flock cackled and chuckled, waving their hooves around.

The caterpillar-chicken-sheep managed to wobble on to her back hooves. She hopped across the field and stood unsteadily in front of the flock, trying to punch her way out of her disguise.

But Shaun had a better idea.

He snatched up a tin opener lying among a stack of baked bean cans. He scuttled back to the caterpillar-chicken-sheep and began to tear holes in the sleeping bag with the tin opener – two for her front hooves, two for her back hooves. Then he stood back. *Ta-da!* The sheep could now wiggle her hooves around with glee!

Suddenly, Shaun heard a rumble. Above his woolly head he saw dark clouds gathering. A rainstorm was coming!

The flock baa-ed loudly and ran for the tent. Nobody wanted wet, wiry wool. Just before the first raindrops fell, Shaun grabbed the caterpillar-chicken-sheep and dragged her into the tent.

Once inside, the sheep huddled closely together. Shaun was surprised – they did all fit in after all! But perhaps the flock was too close for comfort. Shaun heard a rumble that *wasn't* thunder, and a muffled PARP came from the blue sleeping bag.

"Mehh!" the flock bleated and stared in disgust at the 'fowl' farting sheep.

"Maa . . ." she baa-ed sheepishly from inside the chicken. *Sorry!*

Chapter 5
An Unhappy Camper

The rain soon passed, but the sheep were happy to stay where they were. They found plenty to do inside the tent!

After some time, Shaun heard a groan and a grumble outside. The Camper was back, with Bitzer by his side.

The tent door opened with a loud ZZZZZIP and the Camper came face to fleece with the flock. The sheep were reading his paper, twisting his puzzle cube, enjoying hip-hop on his personal stereo and – most oddly of all – watching a raw chicken dancing to the radio!

The Camper gasped and stumbled backwards. The flock ran from the tent, and the Camper could only stare in shock as the caterpillar-chicken-sheep shuffled out behind them.

Then, with a FLUMPH, the tent collapsed.

The Camper roared with rage. This was the last straw!

To make matters worse, Bitzer galloped back to the Camper, with the stick in his jaws. He panted excitedly. *Again! Again!*

No, *that* was the last straw! The Camper snatched the stick and snapped it – THWACK! – across his knee. Then he threw it on the campfire as Bitzer watched in horror.

Bitzer trudged away with a sad "Arooooo!". After all his panting, begging and running, his friend didn't want to play after all. Shaun took pity on the pooch, and patted him on the back.

But as Shaun comforted Bitzer, he kept an eye on the Camper. He was wiggling ropes and kicking pegs, trying to put the tent up again.

Shaun had a brilliant idea. He knew just how to get rid of the rude intruder!

"Psst!" hissed Shaun, and whispered his Grand Plan to Bitzer. The miserable mutt cheered up at once. *Great idea!* Shaun could count on him!

That night, the Camper slept soundly, with his teddy tucked under his arm.

Two shadows – one woolly, one furry – sneaked up outside the tent. One carried a shovel, the other, a spade.

CHUMPF! went the shovel and CHUMPF! went the spade, as Shaun and Bitzer began to dig . . .

The next morning, Bitzer was dog-tired. He yawned as he opened the gate to the field and ticked the sheep off his list.

Shaun? Check.

Shirley? Check.

Timmy? Check.

Caterpillar-chicken-sheep? Check.

The caterpillar-chicken-sheep waddled across the field and landed SPLOOF in a muddy hole! The other sheep stared. *That hole wasn't there before!* Where was the tent?

Bitzer and Shaun looked at each other and winked. They knew *exactly* where the tent was.

Later that morning, the Camper awoke from his deep slumber. He opened the tent door and peered outside.

Something wasn't right.

Where was his box of tasty treats? Where was his campfire and cans of fizzy pop?

The Camper glanced down and shrieked.

His tent was on top of a HUGE pile of rubbish!

Bitzer and Shaun chuckled with glee. Their Grand Plan had worked.

If the Camper wanted to treat his camp like a rubbish tip, he might as well camp *in* a rubbish tip!

WIN WIN WIN!

100s of Shaun the Sheep prizes to be won online!

We're **giving away** Shaun the Sheep books, Nintendo DS games, DVDs, posters, mobile phone skins, charms, toys and much more online.

Remember:
ewe have to be in it to **win** it!

To get your hooves on one of these
sheep-tastic prizes, simply log onto
www.egmont.co.uk/shaunthesheepcompetition
and enter!

EGMONT

E0331